Wild Boys

Previous Books by Rita Ciresi

Female Education (Wordruner, 2019)

Second Wife (Burrow Press, 2018)

Bring Back My Body to Me (eBook, 2012)

Remind Me Again Why I Married You (Delta Publishing, 2003)

Sometimes I Dream in Italian (Delta Publishing, 2000)

Pink Slip (Delacorte Press, 1998)

Blue Italian (Ecco Press, 1996)

Mother Rocket (University of Georgia Press, 1993)

Wild Boys

a novella

Rita Ciresi

Wolfson Press

John Cassels, volume editor
Cover design by Sky Santiago

 First edition.

ISBN: 978-1-950066-26-1

Wolfson Press
Master of Liberal Studies Program
Indiana University South Bend
1700 Mishawaka Avenue
South Bend, Indiana 46634-7111
wolfsonpress.com

Contents

Foreword

PERCEIVING THE DIFFICULTY I WAS HAVING WRITING THIS FOREword, the publisher of Wolfson Press suggested "it could simply convey your reasons for choosing the manuscript."[1] That was helpful but imposed difficulties of its own as those reasons seemed both overdetermined and ineffable as I tried to articulate them. *A* thing I remembered—indeed, I doubt I could forget it—was the moment I knew for sure I wanted the Press to publish *Wild Boys*. Well in thrall to the taut mosaic of Christian Wild's fleet yet unhurried, unerringly paced account of growing up with his twin brother Jordan in a singular family in Lake Forest, Illinois, at about the three-quarter mark I ran smack into a simile of such apt, uncanny power that, to closely paraphrase Seamus Heaney, it caught my heart off guard and blew it open. I was weeping. And though I've since read the book countless times, the crystalizing force of that figurative incident abides.

It is not insignificant that the simile I am here brazenly not quoting—leaving readers to their own experience of it—is phrased in terms of inability, lack of knowledge. Christian is a confident, frequently *very* funny narrator, but a thematic throughline in his telling of his and Jordan's story is anxiety. He

[1] Joe is extraordinarily perceptive, but apprehension of my struggles would not have taxed that power; his reserves of kindness and patience were drawn on extensively, however, and for those I thank him.

worries (among other things) that his family isn't normal, that his parents may get a divorce, about what it means that they are trying to conceive a child as he and Jordan enter their teen years, that in being cast in the familial role of "good" son (" . . . Aeschylus to [Jordan's] Aristophanes, Gallant to his Goofus . . . ") he is somehow aligned "against" the brother with whom he is growing up "like an only child split in two."

The split registers along multiple axes, the behavioral being only the most overt (onset: puberty): "our hormones kicked in and—as Dad said—cooperation took the next train out of town. Jordy started giving our parents trouble. Flouting the rules. Mouthing off." As children will—even, perhaps *especially*, ones who are each other's doppelgänger—the boys stake out and/or wind up serving differential functions in the family system. And the understanding that Christian will act as a kind of superego counter to his brother's robust id occasions a surprising revelation that introduces a more subtle—for the book as a whole, crucial—distinction between the twins.

Their mother, Cathy, wonders aloud to Christian if Jordan's behavior might be motivated in part by jealousy:

> Why should Jordy be jealous of me?
> Because Dad favors you.
> I thought it was the other way around.
> Mom shook her head.

Their father, Jon, a classics teacher by training, prizes linguistic skill and thrust-and-parry wit, grounds on which Christian feels he cannot compete with Jordan:

> Although I was pretty good at Latin—and caught on all right with ancient Greek—Jordy absolutely soaked up the language lessons Dad gave us. . . . Beyond [those], both Dad and Jordy loved parodies and wordplay and doggerel verse. Whenever we drove anywhere as a family . . . Dad would catch Jordy's eye in the rearview mirror and they'd start

> trading puns. . . . I didn't have that kind of jokey relationship with Dad.

Christian, in whose narrative hands we have been utterly secure, is (or has been) less than certain of himself as a wordsmith. He's the "favorite" but doesn't feel it.

Toward novella's end, disaster having befallen the Wild family—it is, strictly speaking, no one's fault, but (by characteristically brilliant dint of Rita Ciresi's design) all have behaved around it in ways that make projected feelings of guilt natural—a grief-benumbed Christian finds himself in therapy and on medication. He seems to be benefitting but isn't happy about either, and in the book's penultimate section,[2] his father offers him an out by way of substitute:

> I was thinking, Dad said, maybe it would help you to write about it.
>
> What *it*?
>
> Your feelings. About Jordy. Or about your family that can't *triangulate*—or whatever the fuck else that doctor of yours thinks is wrong with us.
>
> So I don't have to go back to talking to her? I asked.
>
> Not unless you enjoy spilling your guts out.

Jon Wild plants a typewriter ("one that Jordy used to love to peck at") on his son's desk: "I want to hear that typewriter going, he said. For fifteen minutes, half an hour a night." Christian protests that "Jordy was the writer," but the deal is now that *he* will assume that mantle, will effect a writing cure.

There are echoes here of Stendhal ("Twenty lines a day, genius or not") and of Joe Brainard's influential *I Remember*

[2] *Wild Boys* came to us with a subtitle designating its constituent parts as "flash" fictions. Though one of them—the sly, funny "It Ends the Way It Always Ends"—*has* been published as a story, that isn't quite right, nor does calling the parts "chapters" seem correct. With massaging, a few of the others could *perhaps* stand on their own, but they are clearly intended to work in concert (and I've not come up with anything better than "sections").

(prompted in their initial session to tell his therapist something about Jordan, Christian produces a memory-snippet not unlike the ordinary/sneaky-profound entries that make up Brainard's collage-memoir: "Once we tried to catch a fish. With our bare hands. But it was slippery and got away."). We hear nothing of the termination of Christian's therapy, but we know he completes his assignment (would in fact be a candidate for extra credit), and that completion serves roles both in his life and in *Wild Boys* as a narrative object.

The agreement to substitute *writing* for talk and pharmaceuticals amounts to a kind of contract between Christian and his father, and the fulfillment of its terms both vouchsafes the authenticity of Christian's story—not that we've had reason to doubt—and accounts for its material existence. Jordan may have been "the writer" in the family, but Christian has in turn turned himself into no mean one, and an excellent editor to boot: Fashioning the document we have just read from the one he began generating at his father's behest—he calls it a "list" and talks about it in a way that comes to blur the distinction between it and life—had to have involved significant cutting and shaping (to say nothing of low-key idiosyncratic aestheticization. Christian's observation of fictional convention is decidedly partial, but of course *he* isn't writing fiction).

One of the miracles of Ciresi's sympathetic ventriloquism is how she threads the needle of young Christian's half-formed uncertainties and the serenely virtuosic manner of his relation of them as an older narrator. Neither ever seems incredible or strained. Part of the secret is Christian's mostly *not* indulging in the sort of figurative flight I praised at the start of this foreword. His mastery tells in attentiveness, intelligence of structure, unwillingness to put down (or, like as not, leave in) unnecessary words.

Where he *does* allow himself a little metaphorical flash, its power is commensurately heightened. The sneak attack he launches at the end is particularly breathtaking.

Or I should say: *almost* the end. There is an "Epilogue," consisting of the text of a survey letter Christian has filled out, checking one item. For an embarrassingly long time, I was underwhelmed by this conclusion, less than satisfied with it though I had no other suggestion. Something of the functionary inheres in the figure of Completer-of-a-Form, and it is difficult to imagine a *less* writerly form than, well, a *form*. It seemed to me rote, uninspired. But I was wrong. And my failure was one of reading—namely, *failing* to read (a troubling admission for an editor). The temptation to skip over canned language can be great; particularly where such language has not been ratified, the impulse may be overwhelming. But given what we know of Christian's story at this point—as much as we will ever know—the soft drumbeat of his serial refusal to check the line next to each of the letter's first eleven statements amounts to an extended exercise in excruciating honesty, one that becomes increasingly plangent as the statements sink in, as we read the letter just as he did.

It would be difficult to imagine a better ending.

John Cassels
Silver Spring, Maryland

Wild Boys

Brothers

Back before in-vitro fertilization made twins common as chewing gum, heads turned whenever my brother Jordan and I entered the room. Waitresses brought us matching double-wide slices of pie (and charged my father for only one). Teachers doled out A's. Strangers stopped my parents on the street and peppered them with questions: Which boy is older, smarter, easier going? Do they compete for your attention? Do you have a favorite?

Mom and Dad answered: We try not to compare them. They have our undivided attention. We love them both to death.

Mother

The Wild boys—as we were known—were considered double the fun, but never twice the trouble. How do you get your boys to behave? other mothers asked Mom.

We don't let them drink Coke, Mom said. We don't let them watch TV. We send them to Montessori.

Once I heard her say, It helps that they're terrified of their father.

Father

Jordy and I weren't consciously scared of Dad. But we definitely snapped to it when he entered the room. Dad was a big bear of a guy who had grown up boxing and playing hockey without a helmet. He had huge hands—the palms alone were bigger than my face—and Mom hardly needed to plant the idea in our heads that those hands could crush us.

Grandfathers

Twice a year, at Easter and Christmas, we piled into the station wagon and crossed the Canadian border to visit the farm where Mom had grown up. All of Mom's siblings and cousins seemed in awe of this big, bruising American (with a master's degree in classics!) that she had married. But Grandpa Jourdain, a crotchety old man in overalls, dismissed Dad as book smart, not chore smart. Dad couldn't milk a cow, birth a lamb, plow a field.

So: useless.

Dad always seemed relieved when we headed back south to his own father's home. Yet the closer we got to Saginaw, the more his foot eased up on the gas. Saginaw was gray as the inside of a trash can, and Grandpa Wild's dusty, cluttered row house stunk of whiskey and Winstons. Mom and Dad disapproved of the way Jordy and I fried our faces in front of Grandpa's monster black-and-white TV, watching hours of cartoons—Tom and Jerry, Roadrunner and Coyote, Tweety and Sylvester. Grandpa Wild cussed and drank and smoked and always stared at Mom in a way that wasn't polite.

One Christmas Grandpa got up too close to Mom in the kitchen. Dad and Grandpa got into a shouting match and took it outside. Within seconds, Grandpa was down on the ice.

Dad came back in, blood on his knuckles.

Did you just hit your own daddy? we asked him.

When you grow up, he said, do me a favor. Don't follow my example.

To Mom he said, Pack up. We're never coming back to this shithole again.

Babies, Where They Come From

On the ride back to Lake Forest, Jordy and I fell asleep in the back seat. Dad must have carried us into the house because when I woke early the next morning, I still had my clothes on under the bedcovers.

Usually Jordy and I nodded off and came to within seconds of one another. But that morning I got knocked out of sleep when a distant hum shivered the windowpanes and made the floorboards vibrate. Mom and Dad called the 5:30 a.m. from Kenosha *the baby train*—their sly way of hinting that towns with a train passing through early in the morning had a higher birth rate.

The house was freezing because the thermostat had been turned down for days. I padded across the hall in my socks. The door to Mom and Dad's bedroom was open just a crack and my parents were one big lump under the covers.

I knocked.

Dad groaned.

What's the matter, Chrissy? Mom asked. (Later I heard her tell Dad, I knew it was Chrissy. Jordy would have just barged in.)

I'm cold, I said. And the baby train woke me up.

Come here, sweetie.

I went to Mom's side of the bed. But Dad was the one who leaned over and held out his hand to help me under the blankets Mom had lifted, keeping her and Dad under the sheet.

Mom's shoulders were bare.

Where's your PJs? I asked.

Daddy wanted to take them off, she said.

Mommy had no objections, Dad said.

They laughed. So I laughed too, as if I understood what they were laughing about. Yet I must have gotten it on some level because I started peppering them with questions: Does the baby train come every morning? How do you know when it's going to stop for you? Did you have to buy me and Jordy one ticket or two?

Finally, Mom told me, You and Jordy didn't really come on the baby train, honey.

So how'd we get here?

Remember last spring at the farm, when you saw the baby lamb come out of the ewe?

Yuck-o, I said.

Well, yuck-o was the way you and Jordy came out of me.

You mean we were inside of you? I asked. Where inside of you? What were we doing in there? How'd we get there in the first place?

I forget exactly how Mom tried to explain it—something gooey about love bringing two people together—and giving and receiving—that made conceiving a child sound like a round of "Kumbaya" sung in Montessori. But when she described the actual process: Daddy puts his—

Doesn't that hurt? I interrupted.

In a way that feels good.

You mean you like it?

Dad gave off a lazy laugh. I'd say she likes it quite a bit.

Did you have to put it in twice to make twins? I asked.

No, you and Jordy were one baby that split into two.

Did I split into Jordy or did Jordy split into me?

We suspect it was a mutual decision, Dad said.

Did we come out together?

You had to be polite, Mom said, and take turns.

Who came first?

You did. Daddy caught you. He was so busy admiring you, he almost missed Jordy coming out.

Did Daddy admire Jordy?

No, he started crying.

Why?

Jordy's face was blue and Daddy thought he was dead.

How could Jordy be dead if he was just born?

Sometimes babies are born still.

Still what?

Still as in silent. Not breathing.

Like this? I held my breath.

Mom shook my shoulder. Don't do that.

Another train came by—the 5:55—and once again the whole house vibrated.

Now you can go back and tell Jordy where babies come from, Mom said.

Nope, I said. I like secrets.

Dad groaned. You mean we have to have this conversation all over again?

My brother and I grew up like an only child split in two. We did everything together: eat, sleep, get haircuts and vaccines, whack tennis balls back and forth, play recorder duets and four-hand piano. We sat side by side in Montessori and chapel. So I always remembered that half hour spent in my parents' bed as magical, when there was just the three of us together instead of the usual four and my brother kept sleeping and I had my mother and father all to myself.

Train

Mom wanted the baby train to stop just one more time.

I know it's irrational, I heard her tell another mother, but our boys are always together. I'm afraid there'll be a tornado or a car accident and we'll lose both of them.

Loss

Not too much later Dad took Mom to the hospital and brought her back that night. She came in crying and went straight to bed. Dad couldn't peel the bills out of his wallet to pay the babysitter fast enough.

After he hustled the babysitter out the door, he said, Mom lost a baby.

Where'd she lose it? we asked.

She miscarried it.

Like, dropped it?

The baby came out too early and died.

Can we have a funeral?

No funeral, Dad said. Now go tell Mom you're sorry.

We didn't make her cry.

Tell her you're sorry she lost the baby.

Mom was curled up under the covers, wiping tears from her face with a big wad of Kleenex.

What do you two want? she asked.

Dad said to tell you we're sorry.

Well, you've said it. Now get out of here.

We were shocked. Mom never had dismissed us like that before.

We wandered back into the living room.

Why do you want another baby? we asked Dad. What's

wrong with us? Will you make us dinner? We're hungry.

Dad corralled us into the kitchen and began bumbling around like a cartoon bear. He couldn't find a knife. Couldn't spread the peanut butter evenly. Couldn't put together two slices of bread without the sandwich looking all crooked.

What if you died? we once asked Mom. How would Dad eat?

Oh, she said, women would be lining up to feed him—don't you worry about that.

Fear

Some kids are afraid of spiders. Some of deep water. Some of heights. I was terrified of divorce. A good half of the kids at school came from what my parents called *broken homes*. Another quarter of them had dads who worked and lived in Chicago and only came home on weekends.

Our mom and dad were always there for us. Mom made us a huge farm breakfast every morning—pancakes, bacon, eggs, and oatmeal. Then Dad went off to teach and Mom drove us to Montessori. When Jordy and I got home, we sat at the kitchen table, cruising through big bowls of homemade trail mix and plates of oatmeal cookies while Mom fixed dinner, and in the laundry room the washer churned and the dryer thumped. By six Dad had come home from work and we all sat down at the table together—Dad joking around, Mom supervising our manners, and Jordy and I doing exactly what boys were supposed to do: inhaling food like human vacuums. After dinner we sat in the living room. Jordy and I finished our homework. Mom knitted or crocheted. Dad corrected papers. Then we all went to bed.

Our house was safe and warm and comforting. Yet when we were out in public, I sometimes got the same off-balance feeling I got when I stood too close to the edge of one of Lake Forest's deep ravines. Men lunged to open doors for Mom, who had the kind of natural, girl-next-door beauty shown in soap and shampoo ads. Women always stood up straighter when they were next to Dad, who had the rugged good looks featured on commercials for shaving cream and razors.

At the private girls' school where Dad taught Latin and world literature, the gossipers—and there were plenty of them—said our father liked a pretty face. But they also said, With a wife who looks like that, he stays out of trouble.

Marriage

I never gave a second thought to the fact that Mom and Dad celebrated their wedding anniversary in the spring and we celebrated our birthday in the fall. Then one day when Jordy and I hit eleven, we all sat at the table helping Mom sort through a box of photos, and Jordy picked up Mom and Dad's wedding picture showing them standing outside the chapel on the University of Michigan campus.

Hey, Jordy said, the back of this photo is stamped the same year we were born.

So? I asked.

So—idiot—there are tulips in this picture.

Mom blushed.

Dad said, We were waiting for you two Einsteins to do the math.

I turned red. I couldn't believe I hadn't figured it out before. Jordy was so dumb he blurted out, You mean you *had* to get married?

And good thing, Dad said. Because Mom never would have had me otherwise.

Don't be ridiculous, Jon, Mom said. You know I was crazy for you.

Did Grandpa Jourdain come after you with a shotgun? Jordy asked.

Dad winked. I think it was a pistol.

Mom swatted Dad on the shoulder. There was no shotgun or pistol, she said. Dad and I were going to get married anyway. We just moved up the date. Now put those pictures away so we can have lunch.

Over our soup and sandwiches, Mom and Dad acted like everything was normal. To me it was like the whole table had gone slant. I wouldn't have been surprised if the plates and glasses and silverware had crashed to the floor.

I never wanted to think about those tulips again. But Jordy wouldn't let it go.

How did you guys meet each other? he asked.

Mom was in my Latin class, Dad said.

You mean he was your teacher? Jordy asked Mom.

Mom blushed again. At first. Yes.

Gross, Jordy said. You were supposed to *teach* her.

I did teach her, Dad said. Plenty.

Jon, Mom said. Stop.

Dad laughed.

Jordy made a face. You guys look scared in that picture.

If you're not scared when you get married, Dad said, you're not thinking.

And after that, Mom said, you have to stop thinking and just make it work.

Hormones

Right after that episode, our hormones kicked in and—as Dad said—cooperation took the next train out of town. Jordy started giving our parents trouble. Flouting the rules. Mouthing off. Talking back.

Dad once called him *mischief incarnate*. Now he called him *a horse's ass*.

After all those years of no comparison, suddenly there was nothing but: Jordy is our comedian; Chrissy, our philosopher. Jordy is a runaway car; Chrissy, the brakes. Chrissy asks why; Jordy says, Why not?

I was the moon to Jordy's sun, winter to his summer, tragedy to his comedy, Aeschylus to his Aristophanes, Gallant to his Goofus, the right to his left, the right to his wrong.

Go-Between

Aligning with my parents meant I was against my brother. To go against my brother was to go against myself.

I became their go-between.

Please inform your *Doppelgänger* that we're ready to roll, Dad would tell me.

Kindly ask Mr. Hyde if he wants to order Italian or Chinese for dinner.

Are you coming for a walk with me and Mom, or do you need to consult your id?

Mom simply said, I count on you, Chrissy, to make Jordy see sense.

Marital Satisfaction, Lack Thereof

One morning at the breakfast table, Jordy read aloud from the *Chicago Tribune*: A recent study shows having teenagers in the house decreases marital satisfaction by up to 75 percent.

Tell us something we don't already know, Dad muttered.

Mom got this look on her face, like Dad had slapped her.

Why'd you say that? I asked Jordy later.

I was just reading out loud.

You hurt Mom's feelings.

No, *Dad* hurt Mom's feelings when he agreed with it.

The only reason he agreed with it, I said, is because you act like a jerk. I flopped down on my bed. Why do you always have to come between them?

Jordy flopped down on his bed.

Both of us are between them, he said.

Favorite

One morning, after Dad had sent Jordy out of the kitchen for mouthing off at Mom, Mom asked me, Why does Jordy act that way?

I don't know, I said. I'm not him.

Thank God for that, Dad said under his breath.

After Dad had stalked off to work, Mom asked, Do you suppose Jordy's jealous of you?

Why should Jordy be jealous of me?

Because Dad favors you.

I thought it was the other way around.

Mom shook her head.

This was news to me. Although I was pretty good at Latin—and caught on all right with ancient Greek—Jordy absolutely soaked up the language lessons Dad gave us. I could tell Dad was thrilled that Jordy was a whiz kid in his chosen subject matter. Beyond the dead languages, both Dad and Jordy loved parodies and wordplay and doggerel verse. Whenever we drove anywhere as a family—Jordy sitting behind Dad and me sitting behind Mom—Dad would catch Jordy's eye in the rearview mirror and they'd start trading puns:

Two silkworms had a race. They ended up in a tie.

Two hats were hanging on a hat rack in the hallway. One hat said to the other, You stay here; I'll go on a head.

Two hydrogen atoms met. One said, I've lost my electron. The other asked, Are you sure? The first replied, Yes, I'm positive.

I didn't have that kind of jokey relationship with Dad. I always aligned more with Mom, and this made me nervous because I thought it made me more like a girl than a boy. Or as Jordy would have said, *a faggot.*

Latin Lessons

Dad had gone to Catholic school and had suffered through all the dull stuff served up in standard Latin classes, from Cicero to Beda Venerabilis. To keep us interested in the classics, he gave us the bawdiest works of Juvenal and Martial to translate, as well as much more emotionally charged works like Catullus's "Farewell, My Brother" (which Jordy rendered as *Buh-bye, bro'! I'm still breathing, but you, poor sucker, are dead*).

Mom held her tongue until Dad gave us Ovid's *Ars Armatoria*, which offered long lists of how to find and seduce a girl.

When we got to the line that read *Women can always be caught, that's the first rule of the game*, Mom frowned. When we reached *She'll make you think she means no, while she is planning her yes*, she asked Dad to step into the bedroom.

There we heard her scolding him. What are you thinking, Jon? They are fourteen years old. They don't need any more fuel on the fire.

And him cajoling her: What would you give them—*Phillipics? Epistles?* Loosen up, Cat.

Farmers' Daughters

Dad was conflicted about how to be a father. On the one hand, he knew he needed to be the disciplinarian. On the other, he didn't always want to play the enforcer. He found his "in" with us by doing guy-things and excluding Mom. So the lewd poetry. The secret sessions in the gym, where he taught us how to spar with the punching bag. Our Saturday morning trips to the barber, where he took advantage of Mom's absence to tell jokes about farmers' daughters.

The most memorable one ran like this:

Once there was a farmer with three daughters. When they got old enough to date, he started answering the front door with a shotgun.

One Friday night there came a knock at the door. When the farmer answered—holding his gun—the guy at the door said, Hello, my name is Eddie, I'm here for Bettie, we're going for spaghetti. Is she ready?

The farmer paused, then said, She's ready. For spaghetti.

Another half hour. Another knock. The guy at the door said, Hello, my name is Joe, I'm here for Flo, we're going to the show. She ready to go?

The farmer paused again. Yup, she's ready. For the show.

A half hour later, another knock. The guy at the door said,

Hello, my name is Chuck—

Without pause, the farmer shot him.

Jordy and I thought that was hysterical. Whenever we saw a halfway good-looking girl—which was about every other second since we lived on the campus of a girls' school—Jordy whispered to me, Hello, my name is Chuck.

Changes

At fifteen came the perfect storm: Dad got promoted. We moved into a new house and enrolled in a new school. And along came two new girls who knocked our whole world topsy-turvy.

At Victoria Worth School for Girls, Dad had started out as a lowly language teacher. Slowly he rose through the ranks: head of foreign languages and literature. Director of humanities. Head of faculty. Dean of students. Interim head of school. Finally—and Dad said it was only because the devil the faculty knew was deemed better than the devil they didn't—he was named head of school.

At first Dad looked uncomfortable with his new role. Then he just looked busy. He was always at the office. Or at a board meeting. Or dining with a donor. Or showing his face at a fencing match.

Jordy started making noises about being a fatherless son.

Don't be foolish, Mom said. Your father has to attend school events. Besides, do you think he enjoys dealing with all these headaches? He's made a lot of sacrifices for you. Don't you realize how much it's going to cost to send the two of you to college?

It was understood that Dad, who'd had to attend Catholic college on scholarship, wanted us to enroll in his dream school:

the University of Chicago. Once we finished Montessori (where we'd already skipped two grades, putting extra pressure on Dad to come up with our college tuition), Dad finagled us scholarships to Lake Forest Academy.

Academy kids lived down the street from us, but they might as well have lived on another planet. Their houses were so large they had intercoms. Their fathers understood the commodities market. Their mothers did lunch. Academy girls—half a foot taller than us—wore North Face jackets with ski lift tickets hanging off their zippers. They didn't just ski at Vail; they took to the slopes at Jackson Hole and Snowbird and—as Jordy put it—*fucking Switzerland*. As for Academy guys—who were twice our size—not only could they drive but they drove Jags and BMWs and even Alfa Romeos. On weekends, Academy kids had parties where, it was rumored, the guys tossed their car keys into a bowl and each girl picked out a key and let the owner of the key *chuck* her.

Jordy and I spent hours discussing these so-called key parties. Several obstacles stood in the way of our attending:

1. We weren't invited.

2. We weren't old enough to drive.

3. Even if we could have driven to the party, we would have driven together. So that meant the two of us either would have to toss a coin to see who got to chuck the girl—or we would have to chuck the same girl. But would she let both of us chuck her? If so, which one of us would get to go first?

I wanted to go first. Yet what if I didn't chuck her right? What if I went second, and afterward the girl told me Jordy had chucked her better?

Mom knew nothing about these parties. Still, I overheard her tell Dad, I have a bad feeling about this school. I just think someone—and we all know who—is going to get himself into trouble.

Suspension, Disbelief

The very next day, one of the Wild boys ended up in the headmaster's office. The secretary called Mom and told her, Your son has been suspended from school. No, for fighting. Yes, fist fighting. You'll have to discuss that with the headmaster, ma'am. Please come pick him up.

When Mom arrived twenty minutes later and saw me sulking in the office chair, she blinked. Where's Jordy?

In math class.

You got into the fight? Her incredulity gave way to anger. Go get in the car. Right now.

Wait, where are you going? I asked.

To apologize to the headmaster for your barbaric behavior.

I slunk out to the car. When Mom came back, I expected her to dress me down: What had I been thinking? Dad had pulled a lot of strings to get us into this school! We were there on scholarship! What would a suspension look like to the University of Chicago admissions officers?

Instead, she drove back to Worth School in stony silence and pulled up in front of the administration building.

Get out, she said. Your father is handling this.

Slowly I got out and dragged myself into my father's office. Dad sat at his desk, signing off on some letters. He put down his pen, then he too blinked.

Chrissy? he asked. What are you doing here?

I was the one who got into the fight.

Dad gave me a look that warned, *This had better be good.*

Close that door, he said, and sit down.

I closed the door and sat.

Well?

Silently I debated how much of the following to tell Dad: Jordy and I had been in the locker room when the taunts started. Hey, Wild boy. Wild boys. You pretty boys ever kiss the same girl? You pretty boys ever kiss girls at all?

This guy called Jordy a fag, I told Dad. So I punched him.

How hard?

Black-eye hard.

Dad considered that for a moment, suppressed a smile, and picked up his pen.

Dismissed, he said.

I couldn't believe my luck. I practically floated home.

Well? Mom asked when I sauntered in. What did Dad say?

Nothing.

What do you mean, nothing? What's your punishment?

I didn't get any.

My mother pressed her lips together. Not if *I* have anything to say about it. Keep your jacket on. You're going to rake up all those leaves in the front yard.

But Mom. It's fall—the leaves are just going to keep falling.

Yes, and over the next three days—while you're on suspension—you're going to rake and bag up every last one. After that, you're going to split wood. And clean out the basement and help me haul all that junk to the dump.

That day I raked and split and hauled until my arms felt ready to fall off. My only consolation came at dinner that night when Jordy bragged to my father, You shoulda seen it, Dad. Chris punched this guy's lights out.

Moms and Dads

After that, Academy guys accepted us, and Academy girls adopted us as if we were their little brothers. To boost our cool factor, Jordy put a spin on our comparative poverty. We live in the Dark Ages, he told our classmates. We don't have a TV. Our parents listen to vinyl. Our dad chops wood. Our mom bakes pies.

Pretty soon guys wanted to come over to examine the vinyl and taste the pies. Mom and Dad always invited them to stay for dinner. After dinner, as we messed around with a football or a Frisbee on the lawn, these guys said stuff like: You guys are so fucking lucky. You have *parents*. We have servants.

New House

When Dad became head of school, we moved into the headmaster's house. Willow Cottage was a Craftsman bungalow. The bathroom that Jordy and I shared backed up onto Mom and Dad's bathroom. If we didn't close the bathroom door—and they didn't close theirs—sound from the bedrooms traveled through the vents.

That fall the heat hung on into September, and Mom—usually all over us to conserve energy—never scolded us for constantly running the window AC. Then the first blast of cold air came through, and one morning a thud—like snow sliding off the roof—woke me up. My mother's voice, thin and stretched, came through the bathroom vent: Oh God, Jon, oh God, yes.

I prayed Jordy would keep on sleeping. But within seconds he was sitting up in bed—like a vampire rising from a coffin—and asking, Is that what I think it is?

I put the pillow over my head. I could still hear everything

I didn't want to hear—the bedframe creaking, the headboard thumping, and worst of all, Jordy's assessment of our parents' performance: Wow, Dad's really knocking it out of the park. Whoa, Mom's a total slut for it.

Jordy got out of bed.

Where are you going? I asked.

I'm hungry.

Don't go into the kitchen now, you dumb fuck. Wait 'til they're done.

Hell-bent on being a jerk, Jordy went into the kitchen—which backed up on my parents' bedroom—and turned on the light. He clattered the cereal bowls and clinked the silverware. He came back into our bedroom eating a bowl of Wheaties and reported, A satisfactory conclusion has been reached.

A few minutes later the 5:55 train clanked through downtown Lake Forest and our alarm rang. After I got dressed and went into the kitchen, I noticed Jordy had been stupid enough to leave on the light.

Mom—raised on a farm and accustomed to getting up early—was always the first one in the kitchen. But that morning only Dad, looking disheveled in a T-shirt and sweatpants, came out of the bedroom as Jordy and I sat scarfing down our cereal.

What are you doing up so early? Dad asked.

We were hungry, Jordy said. You?

That *you?*—delivered with a dollop of sarcasm—irked Dad.

Did I invite you to comment on my personal life? he asked. When Jordy made a face at me that Dad thankfully couldn't see—or he would have kicked Jordy's butt clear to downtown Chicago—Dad glared at me. How about you—any jackass remarks you'd care to make?

No, sir, I said.

I could tell Dad was mad at himself for jumping on me when he should have gone strictly for Jordy. But he was too pissed to apologize. Get dressed, he said. This morning I'm driving you two little shits to school.

Mom supposedly was sleeping in, but really she was lying in bed giving Dad instructions: Double-check they have all their homework. Make sure they make their beds. Their lunches are on the second shelf of the refrigerator.

As if Dad were incompetent. Which, truth to tell, he sort of was. He couldn't figure out where things were. Or what steps to take to get us ready for school. Or the right order to do it all in. We got so behind that Dad tossed Jordy the keys and told him to go warm up the car.

Jordy and I had just gotten our learner's permits and loved nothing more than wielding the car keys. That Dad had given Jordy the keys only pointed—to me, at least—to the fact that *Jordy* was his favorite.

On my way toward the back door, I passed Mom and Dad's bedroom. Dad—who was in the bathroom—had left the bedroom door ajar. It seemed rude to just go by without saying anything. I was about to call out, Later, Mom, when she beat me to the punch.

Chrissy, she said, come give me a kiss goodbye.

I so totally didn't want to go into my parents' bedroom. It was dark. And smelled like sweat. My mother's hair was down, and her shoulders were still covered with a nightgown (which made me think: Jesus, had Dad just pulled up her nightgown and given it to her while she was dressed?). There was a thermometer on the nightstand—God knows what they were using that for—and when I looked at it, Mom seemed embarrassed.

Dad and I are trying for another baby.

Jordy would have said something snide. Like: So we heard.

I said, Good luck, Mom.

Thank you, sweetie. You're the best.

She scooted up to give me a kiss.

Suddenly I felt a hand on the back of my neck.

Into the car, lover boy, Dad said, stooping down and stealing the kiss that Mom had meant for me.

Infertility

Probably because we had overheard the act, Jordy and I were convinced that Mom would get pregnant. Yet no happy announcement was made. Mom grew short with us. Dad was on edge. Vials lined up in the refrigerator. Syringes in the bathroom. Doctor's appointments got posted on the calendar. And a stack of bills mounted on Dad's desk. A thousand here. Three thousand there. As Jordy put it: they were flushing our college tuition down the toilet.

Whose fault do you think it is? Jordy asked me.

Mom's the one who had the miscarriage, I said.

Yeah, but Dad is old. Like, forty. He probably gave her VD.

Where would he get VD?

I don't know. A whore or something.

Dad doesn't go to whores.

Maybe he did before they got married. Or maybe Mom slept around.

Don't be stupid, I said. Mom was a virgin when they got married.

How could she be a virgin, Jordy asked, if she was pregnant with us?

I mean she never did it with anyone else but Dad.

How do you know? Jordy asked.

She would never.

Should I ask her?

If you want Dad to pulverize you.

Think he wants to?

What, pulverize you?

No, do it with a woman besides Mom.

My stomach hurt. Jordy had this way of asking questions so the only answer seemed to be *yes*.

Limericks

Jordy made up dirty limericks about our parents:

There once was a couple named Wild
Who valiantly tried for a child . . .

In Jordy's poems, Mom was a farmer's daughter. A Canadian maiden. A Lake Forest strumpet (whose husband most valiantly pumped it). Dad was a boy from the altar. A headmaster from Saginaw. A Latinate fool (with a monstrous tool). These lads and lassies and horndogs and hussies were always discharging their conjugal duties or exploring the state of the union. The lack of results only led them to wonder:

Something must be amiss
With my genital abyss!

or

Whatever could be wrong
With my A-plus-rated dong?

The limericks often ended on a light-bulb moment: Dad discovered his dick was made in China. Mom realized she had accidentally sewn up her vagina.

Every once in a while, I told Jordy to knock it off. Most of the time, though, I just laughed at his limericks. I knew this wasn't normal, to be so aware of our parents' comings and goings (or what Jordy called their *Arabian nights* or their *appointments in Samarra*). Poking fun was the only way to deal with it.

Snow

Post–New Year, Mom and Dad consulted the calendar and made last-minute plans to get away for the weekend. (Wonder why, Jordy commented.) Friday morning it started to snow—icy flakes that stuck the moment they hit the ground—and by afternoon it was coming down so hard it was blinding. Friday night was a complete white out. Saturday morning it was clear that the blizzard had boxed us in.

After breakfast Dad sent us out to shovel the front walk and driveway. Don't come back in, he said, until you've got it all cleared.

What if we have to piss? Jordy asked.

Write your name in the snow, Dad told him.

What if we have to poop?

Do it like a dog. Now get outside before I lose my temper.

Jordy and I pulled on our boots and down jackets. We must have spent over an hour out there, pitching heavy wet snow from side to side while Mom and Dad went back to bed.

Or at least we thought they went back to bed. Between shovels, Jordy kept asking me, Think they're mid-coitus right now?

I don't know, I answered. Who cares? Whatever.

I'm just saying—

Stop saying and shut up.

I didn't want to picture our parents following the instructions provided in the fertility clinic handbook (which Jordy and I had studied with much more interest than our calculus): *To ensure complete ejaculation, the penis should remain inside the vagina until complete detumescence. Post-ejaculation, manual (not oral) stimulation of the woman to orgasm is recommended; the resulting vaginal contractions will assist in drawing sperm into the uterus.*

For lunch Mom fixed us waffles. After lunch, Dad followed us back into our bedroom.

I need you two to make yourselves scarce this afternoon, he said.

What for? Jordy asked.

Do I have to spell this out for *you*? Dad asked me.

No, sir, I said.

Then explain to your bonehead brother—after I leave the room—why I need you to clear out of here.

But Dad, Jordy said. There's like two feet of snow on the ground.

I'm aware of that.

So where are we supposed to go?

My office.

We have homework.

So do it there. And stop giving me mouth about it.

Jordy and I shoved our books in our backpacks, pulled on our still-wet jackets, and trudged across campus, our boots sinking almost knee-deep in the snow.

Jordy grumbled, Whadda they need another kid for when they have us?

Mom wants a girl.

No, *I* want a girl.

I kept quiet. I knew exactly which girl he wanted—and to hide my own much more shameful crush, I pretended I wanted Jordy's girl just as much as he did.

When we got close to Dad's office, Jordy took a left turn.

Where you going? I asked.

Library.

I stopped dead in my tracks.

You comin'? Jordy asked.

What're we gonna say if Dad finds out?

Tell him we had to look up stuff for our paper on *1984*.

Dad had made it crystal clear that the school library was off limits. I followed Jordy anyway.

Worth Girls

Unlike the girls at Lake Forest Academy, who treated us like pet poodles, Worth School girls looked at us like we were real boyfriend material. Every Sunday Mom and Dad dragged us to chapel, and there we heard the girls whispering: Which of Mr. Wild's sons is cuter? nicer? funnier?

At first when Dad noticed them scoping us out—and us scoping right back—he seemed amused. Then concerned. Only after we volunteered to attend a choir concert did he call us out.

I'm assuming your interests, he said, lie well outside the choral works of Dieterich Buxtehude.

We just want to hear the girls sing, Jordy said.

Let's get this straight right now, Dad said. As long as I'm head of this school, you will not look at any Worth girls. You will not talk to any Worth girls. You will not get involved with any Worth girls.

But Dad, Jordy said. Worth girls are into us.

The last thing I need is *you* getting into *them*. Admire from afar.

Penelope

Penelope got parked at Worth School in her senior year while her dad, who had something to do with Standard Oil, worked in Chicago. Penelope had a triple-barreled Venezuelan last name a mile long—like something from a Monty Python sketch—which led Jordy to nickname her *La Zuela*.

Dad called her *out of your league, pal.*

Mom christened her *a bombshell.*

Penelope was so *hello-my-name-is-Chuck* that at first neither Jordy nor I could look her in the eye, so we ended up looking down at her feet. That got us into even more trouble.

Female Footwear

Once Jordy and I were sitting in the kitchen idly speculating about what kind of signals girls threw off when they were interested.

Dad came out of his study and poured himself a cup of coffee.

Look at their shoes, he said.

Hunh? Jordy said.

Look at the kind of shoes a woman has on, Dad said, and you can tell if she wants it.

Jordy snorted. Mom wears *clogs*.

Dad frowned. She doesn't wear them to bed, jackass.

Dad was probably yanking our chains, but Jordy and I felt like he had given us the word of God. For days afterward, we did nothing but stare at girls' feet. We saw only Tretorns and Keds and jelly shoes. Nothing even remotely encouraging.

But then along came Penelope, who wore exactly the kind of leather boots that made me think, So *that's* what Dad was talking about. The toes came to a point. The heels were so high and sharp, you knew it would only take one hand on her shoulder to knock her off balance. And once you got her down, you'd know exactly what to do.

Or not.

Hannah

Penelope had only one friend at Worth School: our cousin, Hannah.

We first met Hannah—whom Mom and Dad called their niece even though she was the daughter of one of Mom's cousins—on one of our annual visits to Grandpa Jourdain's farm. Hannah—six years old to our four—took us out to the barn where the sheep were groaning and bleating. Our initial conversation followed kid logic:

I'm Canadian, she said.

We're American, we said.

I speak English and French.

Eway eakspay igpay atinlay!

I go to church.

We go to chapel.

I have a Tomagotchi.

We have a penis.

No. We had two penises. We unzipped and showed her, hoping she would reciprocate and show us her weewee. Instead, she merely regarded our puny tools with disdain.

My horse has bigger, she said.

Go ride him, then, Jordy said.

Jordy and I zipped up and spent the rest of the afternoon jumping off the loft into the hay.

We only saw Hannah two or three times after that before tragedy struck. The year she turned seventeen, Hannah's parents were driving home from a funeral when they skidded on black ice and ran into a tree. They were killed on impact. Mom's family conferred about the best course of action, and it was decided that Hannah would be sent down to us so she could attend Worth School on scholarship.

Mom and Dad picked up Hannah at the airport and brought her back to our place for dinner.

Hannah's here, Mom called out.

We came out of the bedroom. There stood this tall, beautiful girl, dressed in a black turtleneck and black jeans, with brown hair that went down to her waist.

Jordy and I hadn't expected tall. Or good-looking. And we sure as hell hadn't expected such wondrous tits.

Hi, we said, our eyes more on her sneakers than her face. As Mom and Dad had carefully instructed us, we mumbled our apologies about her parents and told her we hoped she would like living in Lake Forest.

Hannah had lost all her childhood bossiness. She was quiet—and sad—and said, Thank you for adopting me.

You *adopted* her? Jordy blurted out.

Mom looked appalled.

Mom and I are acting as Hannah's guardians until she comes of age, Dad said. Now go set the table.

Jordy and I set the table and we all sat down to dinner. Or rather, Dad, Jordy, and I sat down. Hannah—who obviously had grown up waiting on men, same as Mom—kept getting up to help Mom serve. Every time she rose from her chair to fetch more potatoes or green beans or chicken, I got stiff just looking at her ass.

Afterwards, Mom and Dad walked Hannah back to the dorm to help her get settled.

Think she's hot? Jordy asked me.

Nah. You?

Hell no—she looks like Mom. I'm taking a shower first.

Jordy took such a long shower that I got left with nothing but lukewarm water. Still, I took an even longer shower than he did, prompting him to call out, Did you whack off *twice*?

As I toweled off, I felt guilty and ashamed. I must be a perv, I thought, to imagine banging a girl who looked like my own mother. But then I remembered that plenty of famous men had gotten it on with their cousins: Franklin Delano Roosevelt, Charles Darwin. Jesus, even Einstein! So maybe I wasn't a perv. Maybe I was, like, some kind of genius.

The Daughter They Never Had

Hannah—whom Dad called *statuesque*—was easily the tallest and one of the prettiest girls on campus. Yet she held the same position at Worth School as we held at Lake Forest Academy: she was a fish out of water, a farm girl surrounded by city slicks, a scholarship student. Some girls were nice to her face—after all, she was considered Dad's niece—but they were mean behind her back. Others sucked up to her because they wanted to get to us: Hannah, invite your cousins to the bonfire. Hannah, tell your cousins to meet us downtown on Saturday night. Hannah, sneak your cousins into the dorm.

Hannah no sooner would have thought of defying our mom and dad than she would have considered posing nude for *Playboy*. She worshiped our parents. Every other thing out of her mouth—to us at least—was *Aunt Cathy and Uncle*

Jon. Aunt Cathy and Uncle Jon say . . . Aunt Cathy and Uncle Jon wouldn't want you to do that . . .

Mom and Dad, in turn, were smitten with her. She became like the daughter they'd always wanted. It didn't take long for Mom to start holding up Hannah as an example. Hannah sits still at the dinner table, she chided us. Hannah never tells dirty jokes or uses bad language.

I always had a nagging fear that although I threw Jordy off the scent—and Mom still hadn't caught on—Dad somehow knew I had the hots for Hannah.

Mom and I expect you to show Hannah every respect, Dad told us. You're not to pester her, interfere with her studies, or take advantage of her position. Just in case you choose not to understand what I'm telling you, I've instructed her to tell me if you do anything out of line with Worth girls.

It didn't take long for Jordy to start calling Hannah *Little Miss Tattle-Tale*, *Little Miss Future Librarian*, *Little Miss Prissy-Puss*.

Hannah's tits would probably fall off, Jordy said, if she knew Mom rode Dad like a horse.

Hannah and Penelope

It was natural that if Jordy liked a girl, I'd like the same one. So I let Jordy and everyone else think we both had the hots for Penelope. It wasn't hard to do. Just like me and Jordy, Hannah and Penelope were always together. They were both senior transfers. Both Catholic. Both über-studious. Both brunettes in a sea of blondes. Their dorm rooms were side by side. Where one went, you'd find the other.

That's exactly what I had in mind that afternoon when Dad banished us from the house and Jordy headed for the school library.

The library, which the campus handyman had unlocked for the girls, was hot and stuffy and mostly empty. There was no adult on duty—only a sign posted that said IN THE ABSENCE OF THE LIBRARIAN, CONDUCT YOURSELF WITH HONOR.

Jordy gave the sign the finger and strode in. Sure enough, Penelope sat at one of the tables by the window in her dominatrix boots. Right next to her sat Hannah in her farmyard rubbers.

Tracking snow all over the carpet, Jordy strolled up to their table and set down his backpack. Penelope moved her books to make room for us. However, Hannah looked as shocked as if we had whipped out our penises all over again. She folded her arms across those tits that I was dying to touch.

You're not supposed to be here, she said.

Says who? Jordy asked.

Uncle Jon.

Actually, our dad—Jordy leaned heavy on the *our*, as if to lock Hannah out—told us to come here to study.

What for?

So he could knock up our mom.

Penelope looked puzzled. What is this *knockup*? she asked Jordy.

You know, Jordy said. Put a bun in her oven. Get her in the family way. Impregnate her.

Preg finally got Jordy's point across. Penelope put her hand up to her mouth to hide a giggle. Hannah sat there, furiously blushing.

I'm going to call Aunt Cathy and Uncle Jon, she said.

Don't bother, Jordy said. They take the phone off the hook when they do it.

Jordy wasn't lying. Mom and Dad always left a trail of evidence after they *addressed the state of the union*. A wineglass sat on the nightstand. The bedspread was rumpled. The phone jack got left exposed—for hours—because Dad forgot to plug it back in.

I could tell Hannah was trying to decide which was the lesser of two evils: calling my parents or just tolerating our presence at the library table. She picked up her pencil and bent her head back over her chemistry workbook.

I sat opposite Hannah and started doing calculus. Or tried to do calculus. The thought of Hannah's legs—and my legs—under the same table was giving me a stiffy. Meanwhile Jordy was practically playing footsie with Penelope.

Jordy started writing notes to Penelope on graph paper. At first Penelope smiled and showed the notes to Hannah, who kept frowning at Jordy. Penelope then started writing back without letting Hannah in on it.

Jordy and Penelope were deep in the moment. I was in several places at once. I was puzzling over inverse trigonometric functions. Conjugating French verbs. Reading the rat scene in *1984*. Yet all the while I kept thinking, Now Dad and Mom are . . .

The clock inched forward. Surely Round One was already over. But how long did Mom and Dad have to wait between doing it? And what did they do during the break? The fertility handbook said: *To optimize pregnancy, the woman should lie still with her legs elevated for half an hour*. During that half hour, did Dad lie next to Mom and tell her he loved her? Or did he get up and pay the electric bill?

At 4:30, Penelope and Hannah packed up their books.

Where you goin'? Jordy asked.

To get dressed for dinner, Hannah said.

Jordy was thinking the same as me: To get dressed, first you had to undress. The minute they left the library, he piled up his books.

Where you going? I asked.

You know, and you're coming with me.

I looked again at the clock. Since I wasn't keen on walking in on Mom and Dad *in flagrante delicto*, I stuffed my books in my knapsack. Jordy and I trudged back through mountains of snow. But instead of walking in front of the dorm, we took a detour and went behind.

Behind the dorm lay a ravine so deep that if you fell in it might be months before someone would find you. Since a Worth girl once had committed suicide by jumping in, the ravine itself was fenced off, and the chain-link was masked with bushes covered with red berries that squished like blood all over the snow if you stepped on them.

Jordy and I knew which room belonged to each girl because Dad had the roster posted in his study in case of emergencies. Hannah was in Room 9. I pretended—like Jordy—to be obsessed with Room 11.

We tried to tread through the snow quietly. But Jordy let out a whoop when he fell into a snow bank waist high.

Hannah, thank God, didn't come to her window. Maybe she was in the bathroom. Penelope, however, looked out her window, gave us a saucy smile, and pulled the blinds shut.

Fuck, Jordy said.

We'd been foiled. Now we were covered with snow—and wet and cold—and had no choice but to trudge home.

Jordy stomped his boots on the front porch, threw open the door, and hollered, We're here!

There was no need to shout. Mom and Dad sat on the couch in front of a roaring fire. Dad had his arm around Mom. Mom had her head on his shoulder.

Dad lifted his whiskey glass in salute. *Ave*, he said. Just in time to shovel the *back* walk.

Bad Behavior

Nothing ever stayed secret for long at a school for girls. Two days later, Dad came home from work and nailed us.

Mind telling me, he said, what you two were doing in the library on Saturday?

Looking up stuff, Jordy said.

What stuff?

Like . . . I don't know . . . who wrote *1984*.

The author's name wasn't on the cover of the book?

George Orwell is a pen name.

I'm well aware of that, you little shit—

Jon, Mom murmured.

—and while we're on the topic of authorship, Dad said, maybe you'd like to explain which one of you two jackasses wrote this and left it in the library.

Dad reached into his jacket pocket and held out a piece of graph paper on which Jordy had written a limerick. I saw only that the end of the last line read *No Lysistrata, she!*

Mom came over and snatched the paper away from Dad. Within seconds her face turned as red as Hannah's had.

That's Jordy's handwriting, she said.

I'm handling this, Dad said.

Mom ignored him. Did you write that to Hannah?

I didn't write shit, Jordy said, to that pious little poopette!

Sensing he was rapidly losing control of the situation, Dad went ballistic. He'd had quite enough of Jordy's smartass remarks! and more than enough of his blatant disrespect! For Christ's sake! Did we not stop to think how our jackass behavior reflected upon *his* leadership of this school? Did we not realize how closely everyone was watching every single move he made? Did we not get that there were faculty members at this school who would do anything to get him in trouble with the school's Board? And did we not know the consequences of writing dirty limericks to a girl whose father owned half of fucking Venezuela?

Dad turned on me. And as for you! You! He pointed right at my heart. You're just as guilty, if not more so, for sitting there and not calling Jordy out on his behavior. I don't want either one of you in that library ever again. And I swear, if I find you within a hundred yards of that dorm, you won't be going to college on my dime.

But Dad, Jordy said. We have to walk by the dorm to get anywhere on campus—

You have to walk by the *front* of the dorm. There's no reason in hell you have to walk in the back.

We weren't—

Cut the crap! Dad said. I have it—from a reliable source—that there were two sets of footprints in the snow in the back of the dorm on Saturday.

Mom took in a horrified breath. Jordan Wild, she said. I am appalled by your behavior. And I'm ashamed of you, Christian. You know better.

Dad grounded us for two weeks.

Later that night Mom lit into Dad. I told you, she said. I told you we should have sent them to Catholic school. I told you not to give them that Ovid. And don't think I don't know about those farmers' daughter jokes. You have only yourself to blame for their bad behavior.

Unclassifiable

Then came the night I can hardly stand to remember. Whenever I think about it, my breath gets caught in my lungs and my heart starts to hurt the way it does whenever I walk too fast in subzero weather. I keep asking myself: Is that what really happened? It couldn't have gone that way. None of us ever would have dreamed of saying such stuff to each other. But that was the way it truly went, right?

Dad came home late that night, wiped out from dealing with some faculty squabbling. Mom reheated some chicken for him. Or maybe meatloaf. Afterwards she fixed him a drink. When he said his neck felt stiff, she rubbed his shoulders.

Jordy and I—who were going stir-crazy from being grounded—rolled our eyes and retreated to our bedroom. A half hour later Jordy came out of the bathroom and said, Another Arabian night.

I shrugged.

They're—

All right, I said. I hear. (Even though I hadn't heard anything.)

Jordy went into his desk drawer and pulled out a flask.

Where'd you get that? I asked.

Swiped it from Dad's file cabinet. Jordy opened the flask and belted some back. Ah, whhhhhh-iskey. Want some?

I hesitated for only a second before I took the flask and poured too much down my gullet. The whiskey was hot and burned my throat. I spit out half of it.

Through the bathroom vent, we could hear Mom mewling like a barn cat.

Jordy grabbed my down jacket.

That's *my* jacket, I said.

Wear mine, asshole. I'm outta here.

Even though it was probably all of six degrees outside, freezing our butts off seemed better than staying there listening to Dad take Mom around the bend. We closed the front door quietly and didn't zip up until we were down the porch. Jordy took a long swig of whiskey and passed the flask to me. I guzzled some more—re-burned my throat—tried not to cough—and passed the flask back to him.

Jordy punched my arm and imitated Mom. *Oh Jon, that feels so good.*

I poked him back and kept up the imitation. *I've been dying for it all day.*

Harder!

Faster!

Higher!

Lower!

Here!

There!

This wasn't normal. We knew it. But it was all we knew.

The last time we'd gone behind the dorm, we'd only gotten a smile from Penelope. On this night we hit the jackpot. Penelope stood in Room 11, with the blinds open, almost as if she were expecting us—waiting to entertain us—in just her underwear. I could not stop staring at her bra. Or rather, the breasts that sat inside the bra, like two big cupcakes on the kitchen counter, slathered with frosting, that you couldn't resist reaching out to—

For a nanosecond—or however long it takes a fifteen-year-old boy to get a hard-on—I completely forgot about Hannah.

Jesus, I said.

Christ, Jordy said. Dare me to knock on the window?

Don't, I said. Dad'll kill you.

That was all the encouragement Jordy needed. He shoved the flask in his pocket, crunched through the snow, and rapped his fist on the window. Penelope whipped around, a scared look on her face. When she cupped her hands against the window and saw it was Jordy fogging up the glass with his breath, she smiled and gestured back to the door. I stared—stunned—as Jordy ran around the side of the dorm without even calling out to me, You comin'?

Penelope put on a bathrobe and disappeared from the window. She must have gone to open the front door of the dorm, because a minute later both she and Jordy were standing in her window. Jordy—who clearly had no idea what to do with Penelope now that he had her—seemed more likely to pee his pants than anything. Penelope was the one who put her hands on his shoulders and leaned in to give him a long kiss.

In the waiting room of our pediatric dentist was a crudely drawn book called *Great Bible Stories*. Every six months as I sat there waiting for my turn in the dentist's chair, I used to stare at the picture of the half-naked Eve making eyes at the snake. When the sight of Eve grew too much to handle, I turned the page and read the story of Cain and Abel.

I never used to understand how Cain could put an ax to his own brother. Now I got it. I felt this insane fury that Jordy had dared to do what I had only dreamed of doing. My dick ached to fuck a girl—any girl—and I wanted to kill my brother.

I can't watch this, I thought. I'll go insane. I was about to turn away when the blinds opened in Room 9. Hannah pressed her face to the glass and peered out toward the ravine. I know she saw me, lurking there in Jordy's jacket in the moonlight, because her face looked just like the painting of the *Mater Dolorosa* in the Catholic church down in Highwood. She was the sorrowful virgin looking down on me, the sinner.

The stars shone bright and moonlight bounced off the snow as I walked around the dorm and slowly crossed the quad. Even more slowly, I trudged back up the court to our house. As I grew closer and Jordy (two minutes later? five? I was too drunk to tell) came up behind me, his breath ragged from running through the cold, the living-room light flicked on in our house.

We're fucked, Jordy said.

No, we're *dead*.

As we walked up the porch Jordy said, You go in first. Dad never gets mad at you.

Bullshit, I said and pushed him so hard through the front door that he stumbled on the rug. It had all been his idea in the first place.

Dad stood by the fireplace. The last time he had railed against us for sneaking behind the dorm he'd had on his headmaster outfit: a wool jacket and tie. Now he had on just a pair of sweatpants and a T-shirt—like he was ready to take on a punching bag in the gym.

He pointed at Jordy. Tell me—right now—where you've been.

Out, Jordy said.

Out where.

Around, Jordy said.

Is that your final answer? Dad asked. Not waiting for a *yes* or *no*, he grabbed Jordy by the arm. You, he said—goddamn you, you stink of alcohol—are coming with me into the kitchen. And you—he pointed at me—get in your room and close the door. Let's see how well your bullshit matches up.

I took my time going into the bedroom. I didn't close the door all the way. Instead, I leaned against the doorjamb, straining to overhear whatever cock-and-bull story Jordy was cooking up. From the way Dad's voice grew more insistent—How many times do I have to tell you to keep away from those girls? That's all I need, for one of you dumb fucks to knock one of them up!—I could tell Jordy wasn't owning up to anything. I also could tell Jordy had said something snarky about Mom and Dad being otherwise engaged, because Dad suddenly grew so furious I was afraid he'd take Jordy out.

Did I solicit your opinion on my relationship with your mother? he shouted. Did I ask you to provide your asinine commentary on what goes on between a husband and wife?

Dad got more and more wound up, until he started to spew stuff that fathers always say: Look me in the eye when you're talking to me. Don't give me that smart-aleck tone. You're living under my roof and you'll follow my rules.

I don't know when I went into the living room to do—what? Stop Dad? Protect Jordy?

Maybe it was when Dad said, How fucking stupid do you think I am?

I don't remember when Mom opened their bedroom door.

Maybe it was when Dad said, My father would have knocked me clear across the room if I had talked to him like that.

According to the fertility handbook, Mom wasn't supposed to get up for half an hour after they made love. But she obviously was scared Dad was going to hurt Jordy, because she had thrown on Dad's bathrobe and was tying the belt around her waist in a hurry.

Jon, Mom called out. Don't.

That *don't* tipped Dad over the edge. All his rage—his frustrations with work, his inability to control us, his inability to get Mom pregnant—balled up at once. He was looking at my mother, but he backhanded Jordy—with his left hand, not his right—so his wedding ring connected with the top of Jordy's cheek. Jordy—dazed—landed against the wall, so hard I took a step back too.

Go back to bed! Dad told Mom. And don't ever *don't* me again.

Mom too stepped back, as if Dad had slapped her, and disappeared into the bedroom. She slammed the door behind her.

I never had seen my father looked scared before. He must have known he had crossed a line with Mom—entered that dangerous territory in which wives told their husbands to pack their bags and take the next Greyhound out of town.

Goddamn you, Dad said to Jordy. Then: Goddamn the both of you. Don't you ever come between me and your mother again.

Jordy and I thankfully got back into our bedroom without Dad crushing us. Jordy—looking, as Dad would say, *less than repentant*—threw himself across his bed and held a pillow against his cheek.

Now I know where you got your punch, he told me. Jesus, this hurts.

Through the bathroom vent we could hear Mom and Dad. Dad was trying to apologize. Mom wasn't having any of it. You promised never to raise a hand against them, she kept saying. You hit Jordy! You hit Jordy, but you were looking at me! No one forced you to marry me! No one held a gun to your head! Whoever stopped you from doing what you wanted to do? You stopped yourself! Walk out, then. Walk out on us. I don't care. Get away from me, don't touch me, if I am pregnant, I swear to God I'd get rid of it, I'd rather die than have another child with you.

In between Dad's apologetic words—and Mom's wild shrieks—Jordy kept up a running commentary: Wow, that's some shit Mom's calling him out on. See if Dad gets laid tomorrow night. Whoa, see if Dad gets laid ever *again*. Would you rather live with Mom or Dad if they get divorced?

Shut up, I said. Because my head hurt from the whiskey and Dad had as good as cursed the day I was born and I didn't want to live at all if it meant I had to choose between living with my mother or my father.

I crawled under the bedcovers in my clothes. Jordy did the same and switched off the light.

Only after it was dark—and Mom had stopped sobbing and Dad's voice had gone silent—did I ask: So did you do it with Penelope?

Jordy laughed. Until she begged for mercy.

Fuck you, liar, I said.

All that night I tossed and turned. Every time I turned onto my left side, I felt my cheekbone ache, as if Dad had caught *me* with the back of his wedding ring.

Morning After

When the alarm jangled, Jordy kept on sleeping. I was so pissed at him I didn't try to nudge him awake. My head felt like it weighed 100 pounds. I wanted to be proud of myself—I had my first hangover!—but all I felt was sick and depressed.

I dreaded going into the kitchen. Whoever coined the phrase *you could cut the tension with a knife* didn't know my parents. A chainsaw would have been the only tool to slice through their anger. Mom stood at the stove—in her own bathrobe, not Dad's—with her back to Dad. Dad sat at the table drinking coffee, fully dressed in his jacket and tie, as if to prove he was in charge again.

Where's your brother? Dad asked.

Asleep.

Get him up.

He'd been talking to me, but Mom was the one who went to wake Jordy. I heard Jordy mumbling some shit, and Mom say, Oh my God, your face, let me see your face—

Mom came back into the kitchen. He can't go to school, Jon—

Oh yes, he can—

—looking like that. Step in there and see what you've done to him.

Dad pushed back from the table and went into our bedroom. I doubt he even looked at Jordy before he shouted, Get up and get your lazy ass to school. I don't want to see you here when I come home for lunch.

Dad didn't kiss Mom goodbye. He didn't clap me on the shoulder. He put on his coat and boots and let in a freezing blast of air as he stormed out the front door.

Mom's lip quivered. She wiped away tears. Then a pulsing, high-pitched squeal caused her to cover her ears. The eggs were burning in the pan and she rushed to turn off the stove and disable the smoke alarm.

Sit down and have something to eat, she told me.

I'm not hungry, I said.

She pulled an icepack out of the freezer and went back in to Jordy. For some reason, I followed her. Jordy, who was just a lump under the covers, was telling her he had a headache and his throat hurt.

Mom put her hand on his forehead and gasped. You're burning up. She got her thermometer—the one she always kept by her side of the bed—shook it down, and slipped it under Jordy's tongue. When she took it out, she frowned. This has to be wrong, she said. She shook it down and put it back under his tongue again.

Do *you* feel sick? she asked me.

I dunno. Sort of.

Mom waited another minute, then looked at the thermometer again. You'd better stay home, she told Jordy.

Mom, I said.

What.

Dad said—

I don't take orders from him.

The last words I ever said to my brother: Fuck you, liar. The last words Dad said: I don't want to see you here when I come home for lunch.

Mom said, Go back to sleep, honey. I love you.

The drive to school was silent as death. Halfway there, Mom let out a strangled noise, pulled over in front of one of Lake Forest's many mansions, put her head down on the steering wheel, and lost it.

I don't know what got into your father, she said between sobs. I don't know what got into me. I can't believe we said such awful things to each other. I can't believe Dad hit Jordy.

I wasn't sure what I was supposed to do—hold her hand? put my arm around her? tell her everything would be all right?

I'm going to be late for English, I said.

Mom gave me this look, like she hated me as much as she hated Dad. She wiped her tears with the back of her glove and resumed driving.

That morning wasn't the first I'd ever been at school without Jordy. Since he'd been born without a spleen—which the doctors discovered only after his appendix almost ruptured—he had always been susceptible to colds and earaches and flu and often was still recovering from whatever illness we both had days after I'd licked it. Still, that morning everyone kept asking me where Jordy was, as if they knew something as bad as that Bible story had gone down:

Then the Lord said to Cain, Where is your brother Abel?

I know not, he replied. Am I my brother's keeper?

In English, we were discussing *King Lear*. In French, we reviewed the pluperfect. In gym, we ran indoor track. I ran and ran, like I could outrun all my problems.

Then I passed out.

The gym teacher sent me to the nurse's office, and the nurse called home. Twenty minutes later, the Worth School handyman—this big guy known as Mr. Z.—was standing in the infirmary.

Your brother, he don't feel so good, he said. Your dad sent me to pick you up.

Mr. Z. looked like he was the one who didn't feel so good. I wondered if he had gotten caught in the middle of something between my parents.

It was snowing—hard—on the way home. Mr. Z. was the first to see the red flashing lights of the rescue truck parked in front of our house. He stopped the car short. I flung open the door and ran out. The EMTs were opening the back of the truck when Dad came sideways out of the door, carrying Jordy—or Jordy's limp body—like King Lear carrying Cordelia.

Dad put Jordy onto the gurney the EMTs had just unfolded and Mom ran out of the house, pulling on her coat. Snowflakes swirled around.

You take Chrissy, she told Dad. I'm going with Jordy.

Dad turned, surprised to see me standing there. He grabbed my arm. Let's go.

It was freezing cold. Dad didn't have on an overcoat. Still, he seemed to be sweating as he pulled me toward the car.

Dad, I kept saying. Dad, what's the matter with Jordy?

He has a fever. A very high fever.

He's going to be all right, right?

Dad didn't say anything. His face looked like stone as he drove on the bumper of the rescue truck to the hospital.

In the ER, only one family member was allowed back with Jordy, so Dad was stuck sitting on the orange plastic chairs with me. He kept cracking his knuckles so hard I felt like my own were going *pop, pop, pop*.

Half an hour later, in the Family Conference Room—where Mom already sat, holding a balled-up Kleenex in her hand—the doctor told us, We'll have to wait for the test results, but it looks like meningitis.

But he's been vaccinated, Mom said.

That isn't foolproof.

But he got the shot, Mom repeated. Last month. They needed it to get into college. They both did.

The doctor turned to me and did a double take. You twins?

I nodded.

You share a room with your brother? Razor? Cup by the sink?

They're twins, Mom repeated. They share everything.

The doctor drew up a chair next to me. How are you feeling right now?

I shrugged. Off.

Headache? Fever?

They sent him home from school, Mom said, her voice growing even more anxious. He passed out in gym.

That's because I didn't eat breakfast, I said.

You weren't hungry this morning? the doctor asked.

I shook my head.

I felt sick to my stomach, I said. Because of what happened last night.

Mom looked down at the conference table. Dad stuck his hands in his pockets and looked out the window.

What happened last night? the doctor asked.

I . . . I . . . got into a fight with my brother.

That's some shiner you gave him, the doctor said.

Something came out of the throat of my father. It wasn't a word. At least any word I recognized. Before he could say anything else, I told the doctor, Yeah, I took a good shot.

The doctor put his hands on my throat. Any tenderness here? Here? Does it hurt if I– ? Open your mouth. Say ah. Louder. Wider.

He turned to my parents. I don't see any evidence of infection here. But let's not take any chances. I'll order a CT scan for him.

Mom started crying. Dad put his arm around her and she didn't resist. The doctor—who probably was used to weeping mothers—pulled a notepad out of his pocket and started shooting off questions. Do you have other children? What school do these two attend? Do they play sports? Is there a girlfriend?

The doctor's pager buzzed. Wait here, he told us. I'll send in a nurse. We're going to need a list of whomever your sons—both of them—have come into contact with in the past 72 hours.

I started to sweat. Mom looked deathly ill. Dad shook like a volcano right before it spewed fire and ash.

Tell me—right now—exactly what you two were up to last night, he said.

I bit my lip.

Chrissy, Mom pleaded, tell Dad. You *have* to tell Dad.

So I told him.

Dad headed for the door. Excuse me, he said. I have phone calls to make.

It Had to Be Jordy

The CT tunnel was so close and cold I felt at first like I was being slid into a freezer. When I started to sweat, I felt like I was being delivered into a crematory oven.

Afterwards there was a lot of waiting. Dad was at the nurse's station, calling our school. Calling Worth School. Calling what Mom called *counsel*.

You mean a lawyer? I asked.

Dad has to report meningitis right away, she said. Otherwise, the school will be held liable if there's an outbreak.

I was sure Dad had already sent someone—like the dean of students—to bring Penelope in for testing.

What about Hannah? I asked Mom.

Hannah? Mom blanched. Did you—or Jordy—touch Hannah?

Mom, I swear I didn't lay a finger on Hannah. I can't stand Hannah—

You have no reason not to like Hannah.

I do too. She called Dad and ratted on us last night.

What are you talking about? Mr. Z. was the one who called Dad. He was unclogging a toilet in the dorm and he said he saw you going down the senior hall—

That was Jordy, I said. He had my jacket on.

—but Dad wouldn't hear it. He said, If it was one of those two going after a girl, it had to be Jordy.

Two Instead of One

We got called back into the Family Conference Room and a different doctor put our scans up on the light box. Your son Jordan, he told Mom and Dad, has inflammation of the brain consistent with bacterial meningitis. We have him in the ICU—

Mom started crying again.

—and we'll treat him with antibiotics. He'll have to fight through the infection.

Dad crackled his knuckles so loud the doctor jumped.

He doesn't have a spleen, Dad told the doctor.

I know. Your wife told me. That's congenital, right? Since his brother—the doctor pointed to the other set of slides—well, congratulations, Christian, I've never seen this before, it's probably one in a million—is polysplenetic. That means you have *two* of them.

Can't you take one of mine, I said, and give it to Jordy?

No, no, it doesn't work that way. The good news is that your scan is completely clear.

Can't you just give Chrissy—I mean Christian—the antibiotics anyway? Mom asked.

Absolutely not. With him—the doctor gestured at me—I would just watch carefully. Take his temperature every couple of hours. Any fever, severe headache, stiff neck, bring him in right away.

Jordy was only allowed one visitor at a time, so Dad let Mom go up to the ICU first.

Mom was up there a long time. Dad kept cracking his knuckles. And pacing. After a while, he said, You didn't have to do that.

Do what?

Tell the doctor you hit Jordy.

It's all right, Dad.

It's not all right.

A nurse came to the door. Mr. Wild? Would you come with me?

Wait here, Dad said.

Dad, I said. Don't leave me here. Why can't I go with you?

Stay here, Chrissy. We can't have you getting sick. It would kill Mom to lose you too.

Maybe just a minute passed—or a whole hour—before my parents returned. Right before they came to the door, I remembered suddenly thinking, Why had Dad said *lose*? And *too*? Had he seen something sorrowful in the nurse's face—the same thing I saw now in my parents' eyes? Had he known even before he went upstairs that Jordy was—?

I knew. I must have known before they even told me, because I could hardly bear to look at my mother when she sat down in the chair next to me and put her hand on my leg and lowered her head, reminding me of that picture in our childhood edition of *Peter Pan* that showed Wendy stooped over her needle and thread. *Don't cry, Peter*, the caption read. *I will sew your shadow back on again.*

Dad knelt beside me, as if he were in church. He took my hand and said, Your brother is dead.

One Instead of Two

In the parking lot, icy pellets were falling. Dad didn't have a coat or gloves. Yet he made me get into the car—Get into the car with your mother, he said—while he scraped the windshield. Mom just sat there in the front seat, like she was frozen. Dad rocked the car so hard with the ice scraper I was afraid it would tip over.

At home a purple crocus had pushed through the snow in the garden. We all stopped and stared at it. None of us wanted to go back inside.

Mom said, I'll make some soup.

Dad said, I'll make a fire.

Neither one of them did what they said they were going to do. They both stared at me, so hard I felt like I was shriveling smaller and smaller, until I was all balled up on the couch and crying like a baby.

Mom, Dad, I said, please, please, *please* don't get divorced.

Oh, Chrissy. Mom sank down on the couch and put her arms around me. Jon, tell him. He needs to hear—

That's not going to happen, Dad said. You have our word.

Afterwards, when we were eating soup (God, how could we have eaten *soup*?), I felt mortified to have bawled like a girl in front of my father.

Wuss, Jordy would have called me. *Pussy*.

I looked at the empty chair at the table and thought, Now Jordy can't say anything ever again.

Angel

Mom and Dad were terrified that our bedroom was infected with meningitis germs. After they made phone call after phone call, I lay down on the couch in front of the dying fire. The embers popped. The light flickered. The clock ticked. Just as I was about to drift off, a tall, white, robed presence entered the living room.

Mom? I whispered.

She went over to the window and looked out on the snow. How can Dad sleep? she said softly. How can Dad snore, when Jordy is dead?

There Once Was a Boy from Lake Forest

In the morning, the phone started ringing, and for days it didn't stop. The school housekeepers—women from Waukegan who made weird clucking noises in their throat to show their sympathy—stripped the sheets off our beds and tossed our toothbrushes and bleached the bathroom surfaces. Mr. Z. took our mattresses to the dump. Mom and Dad, not thinking straight, ordered two new twin mattresses delivered to the house.

Arrangements were made. Who would speak. Who sing. Who act as pallbearers. Who ride in which town car to the cemetery. Who provide the flowers, the food. In the afternoon, Mom told me both Penelope and Hannah had tested positive for meningitis and were isolated in the hospital, but they were expected to be all right.

Do you want to see Jordy, Dad asked, one last time?

I shook my head.

It might help you to say goodbye.

I don't want to say goodbye, I said. I want everything to go back the way it was.

That isn't going to happen, Dad said. You have to accept that.

Jon, Mom said. Don't push.

I'm not pushing, Cat.

You guys said you wouldn't fight, I said.

We're not fighting, honey. We're just trying to do the right thing by you.

In the end I went to the funeral parlor and looked at Jordy. He was lying there, still as some musical instrument I didn't know how to play, resting in a velvet case. Any minute now, I expected him to sit up and say, *There once was a boy from Lake Forest . . .*

There's wax in his nose, I said.

That's embalmment, Dad said.

But there's wax in his nose, I said, can't you get them to take it out? He can't breathe, Dad—

Dad put his hands on my shoulders and turned me away. Mom stayed by the coffin, holding one of the afghans she had knitted for us to take to college.

From the hallway I saw her cover Jordy with the blanket and tuck it in around his body. She leaned over and kissed him on the side of his face where the blood had pooled from the bruise.

On the way out of the funeral parlor, Dad told the director, You can close the lid now.

Farewell, My Brother

The morning of the funeral, Mom straightened Dad's tie, then mine.

Dad put his hand on my shoulder. Let's get this over with, he said.

Just hours before, the campus had been a ghost town—half the girls had gone home at the first mention of meningitis—but now the parking lots were as packed as they were during the annual Christmas party. There even was a cop in the roundabout directing traffic.

Some people stopped when they saw us walking to the side door of the chapel.

Why's everybody staring? I asked.

Get used to it, Dad said.

Inside, the chaplain hugged Mom and shook Dad's hand. The funeral director gave us directions like it was a school play: You will enter . . . the coffin will be carried . . .

Dad looked disgusted, and Mom looked scared that Dad would cuss out the funeral director or the chaplain. Or God.

The only good thing about the funeral was that Hannah was still in the hospital and I didn't have to sit next to her in the front pew.

Dad sat between me and Mom and put his arms around both of us.

Don't cry, I thought.

Then I heard Jordy's voice: *Crying is pussy.*

I held it back until they carried Jordy's coffin up the aisle and parked it right next to me, so close I could reach out and touch the brass handles. I kept thinking of him inside there, with that wax in his nose. Why couldn't the chaplain just open the lid and raise him like Lazarus from the dead?

I started crying so hard that Dad stroked my hair like I was a baby. Mom fed me Kleenex. To stop myself from sobbing, I looked up at the wooden cross of the chapel and prayed to God: Just let me fuck a girl, just once, and I can die after that.

The Ceremony

Music: Pachelbel's Canon. "Ave Maria." "Time to Say Goodbye." *Godspell*'s "Day by Day." (Afterwards Dad said, I could have done without that tambourine.)

Readings: The Lord giveth and the Lord taketh away. All are of the dust. Death be not proud. Do not stand at my grave and weep, I am not there, I do not sleep. *Ave atque vale*: for now and forever, my brother, hello and goodbye.

Breath

Halfway through the reception on campus, Mom told Dad, I can't take this anymore.

Dad opened his mouth to protest, then relented. Walk your mother home, he told me.

Do I have to come back? I asked.

No. Be with her.

Mom and I trudged back through the snow. For the first time all day, I felt like I could breathe.

When we went through our front gate, and Mom saw the crocus, she said, Jordy was walking home with us.

You think?

I heard his breath.

That was my breath, Mom.

I heard his. I know it.

When he finally got home, Dad looked like a wreck.

Mom took his jacket.

Drink? he asked her.

She shook her head.

Chrissy? he asked.

Jon, don't—

Why not? Dad asked. It's not every day you get to bury your own brother.

He took the glass, paused, then hurled it at the wall, where it broke into a thousand slivers.

That night Dad drank himself sick and stumbled off to sleep, mumbling, Can't put this day to bed soon enough.

Haircut

Chrissy needs a haircut, Mom told Dad.

Dad always took Jordy and me to the shop in town, where the same barber did me and him back to back and knew we were double crown, four on the side, two on top. Now in the car with just me for the first time, Dad adjusted the mirror and asked, What do you say we go down to Highwood?

I was relieved. No, thrilled. Like, Dad got it. He didn't want to be stared at any more than I did.

When we walked into the barber shop in Highwood—and the room suddenly went quiet—I got a sick feeling inside. Who should be in the barber's chair but the school handyman, Mr. Z., who obviously had been telling our sad story to the barber and his cronies.

Mr. W., he said when he saw Dad in the mirror. What you doing down here in our neck of the woods?

Dad pointed at my shaggy head. He needs his hair cut.

The barber—this old Italian guy who hardly spoke English—looked at me sorrowfully as he went at my head with the clippers. After he whipped off the cape, he refused to take money from my dad.

On the way out, Dad shoved the ten for my haircut in a charity can for leukemia.

Next time, he said, we go to Waukegan.

Or Wisconsin, I said.

Or Waikiki, Dad countered.

It was my turn. But I wasn't half as quick with words as Jordy had been.

Or, I said, I don't know. Wherever.

Driving home, Dad didn't tell any farmer's daughter jokes. He kept looking in the rearview mirror, where Jordy always sat.

Dad!

What?

You just ran a stop sign!

Fucking hell, Dad said, as flashing lights—and a spurt of a siren—came up behind him.

The cop who approached the car seemed all set to ask Dad for his license and registration until Dad rolled down the window. He stared at Dad, then looked at me like I was a ghost.

Wait a second, he told Dad. I directed traffic at your son's . . . I mean, I'm sorry for your loss.

I'm assuming you didn't pull me over to tell me that, Dad said.

No, sir. You ran a stop sign.

My mind was somewhere else, Dad said.

The cop looked like he didn't know what to do. Warn Dad? Ticket him?

I'll let you go, he said. But you might want to be more careful. Especially with your son in the passenger seat.

After the cop moved away from the car, Dad looked over at me.

Mom doesn't need to know about this, he said.

Angry Gods

No longer were we a family everyone admired. We'd been brought low, as though some angry god had swooped down and lopped us off at the knees. At school, kids steered clear of me, like I carried bad luck as well as meningitis. Mom stopped taking walks. She couldn't bear to go to the grocery store. People either said the wrong thing or, worse, turned away. She donated all seven of the copies she received of *When Bad Things Happen to Good People* to the thrift store. Let bad things happen to someone else, she said.

Mom and Dad became very quiet. Very careful. Very polite. Dad called me Chris instead of Chrissy. Mom didn't make me visit Hannah in the hospital. Nor did she ask Hannah to come over for dinner after she got out. I knew she didn't want to see Hannah sitting in Jordy's chair. I didn't either.

The medicine disappeared from the refrigerator. The syringes went into the trash. The thermometer was back in the medicine cabinet. Nobody talked about having another baby again.

Alcohol

Dad's father was a drunk and Mom was scared Dad would become one too. She silently fretted when Dad came home from school and went straight to the liquor cabinet to fix a drink.

Don't give me that look, Cat, Dad said.

I didn't say anything. Did I say something? she asked me.

And don't put our son in the position of referee.

Mom, I said. Dad. You said you wouldn't fight—!

They both fell silent.

Dad took a belt of whiskey and said, I already told you I'm not going anywhere. The two of you are stuck with me.

Absence, Presence Of

My brother's empty desk. My brother's empty bed. My brother's clothes in the closet. My brother's shoes on the floor. Jordy was there but not-there. At breakfast I took two cereal spoons out of the drawer instead of one. When I set the table for dinner, I pulled down four plates instead of three.

Dad pushed the kitchen table—and Jordy's chair—up against the wall. He pushed our beds together, and the sensation of being only half on a whole interrupted my sleep. I dreamed I was at the cemetery and Jordy was lying in the grave in a bed of snow.

Come on, I said. Get up. We were supposed to be home an hour ago. Dad's gonna kill us.

I woke in a sweat, stuck in the crack between the two mattresses. My body hurt and my head felt stuffed with cotton. It got worse and worse until morning, when I called out to Mom, I can't get out of bed.

And that night they ambushed me.

Mom and I have made an appointment for you to see a doctor, Dad said.

What kind of doctor? I asked.

A counselor, Mom said. Someone neutral to talk to.

You mean a shrink? I said. I don't want to go to a—

You're going, Dad said, whether you want to or not.

But Dad. Mom. You're ganging up on me.

We're not ganging up on you, honey, Mom said. This is for your own good. Can't you see how worried we are about you?

You're going, Dad said. End of discussion.

It Ends the Way It Always Ends

Tell me why you're here, she said.

Because my parents sent me here.

Why did they send you?

To help me handle the situation.

And the situation is?

My brother.

The *death* of your brother.

Something like that, I said.

You seem uncomfortable.

This chair's okay.

Uncomfortable with *me*.

I thought you'd look like my mother.

Why is that.

She listens.

And your father?

He doesn't want to hear it.

What does your father want?

For me to man up.

Which consists of—?

Cracking your knuckles and keeping your mouth shut.

As opposed to—?

Sitting in this chair next to a box of Puffs.

Tell me something about your brother.

He's dead.

Something about when he was alive.

Once we tried to catch a fish. With our bare hands. But it was slippery and got away.

How did your brother die?

Kissed a girl.

Your brother kissed a girl.

I just *told* you that.

Your brother kissed a girl and—?

Got meningitis.

Did you want to kiss that girl, too?

No, I wanted to grind her so deep into the ground we'd both end up in the grave.

Grave is an interesting word.

Grind is even interesting-er.

Why didn't you kiss—or grind—the girl?

He got there first.

You were used to going first?

I was older.

By how much?

I don't know. Two, three minutes. How much longer do we have to keep talking?

Why are you so anxious to leave?

Your artwork is ugly.

Why do you say that?

It doesn't have any people in it. Just colors. So you can't figure out what it's supposed to be about.

What do you think life is about?

Being happy, I guess.

Were you happy before your brother died?

Most of the time.

And now?

Everything's fucked.

Your mother says you're having trouble sleeping. Concentrating. And that the precipitating incident came when your father was trying to teach you how to shave, is that right?

Maybe.

What happened that morning?

I cut myself.

How.

Wasn't looking. The way my dad said I should.

How were you looking, then?

Like . . . like I was getting pulled through the glass, to the other side.

Did you tell your father that?

Sorta.

And what did he say.

Get it together.

Why do you think he said that?

He thinks I'm losing it. I heard him on the phone. I heard him tell you, I just want my son back.

Which son do you think he was referring to?

I don't know. My brother. Me. Both of us, I guess.

You don't think he was worried about you? Concerned about your well-being?

You talked to him. So why do you keep asking me this stuff?

I want to know your thoughts. Your perspective. Your feelings.

Why do I have to feel something about everything? I don't want to have feelings. They don't get you anywhere.

Where would you like to go, if you could go anywhere?

Antarctica. Or some place so cold you couldn't feel your own feet.

Where would you live?

An igloo.

With who?

Just myself, I guess.

What about your parents?

What about them?

Where would they be?

Left behind.

Do you feel left behind?

No. I don't want to go where my brother went.

So you're saying you don't want to die.

Something like that.

You keep looking at the clock.

An hour here isn't really an hour, is it?

Our session is fifty minutes.

So at the end, are you going to say it?

Say what?

I've seen the movies. It starts the way it always starts: *Tell me why you are here*—and ends the way it always ends—*I'm afraid our time for today is up.*

Aftermath

Mom had dropped me off at the shrink. Yet Dad was the one waiting in the parking lot, staring out the windshield like the car was never going anywhere ever again.

He blinked—and looked away—when I got in.

Well? he asked.

I tried to figure out what my father really meant: *Are you cured?* or *Was the shrink worth looking at?*

Mom's prettier, I told him.

That seemed man enough.

Drugs

I gave the prescription the doctor had written for me to Mom, not Dad.

I put the pills on your nightstand, she said.

I don't want to take them, I said.

The doctor thinks—

I don't care what the doctor thinks.

Dad and I think—

I don't care what you think either!

Mom got tears in her eyes. Either you do as I tell you, she said, or you'll have to have this discussion with your father.

I went into the bedroom and swallowed a pill. It tasted metallic.

Family Dynamic

Over the next few sessions, the shrink asked fewer questions about me—fewer questions about Jordy—and started harping on Mom and Dad's behavior. Would you say your parents have a happy marriage? Do they show each other affection? How long had they been trying to conceive? Did it bother you to overhear them having sexual relations? Did you feel threatened by the possibility of their having another child? Do you think your brother felt threatened? Would you call your parents exhibitionists? Did they ever use you two as their audience?

She said she thought our family operated on inclusion and exclusion; Jordy and I performed for Mom and Dad, and they performed for us. Now, without Jordy, we had an inability to *triangulate*. It would be beneficial for all three of us to meet.

At the next session, my parents sat on the doctor's couch—where I usually sat—so I sat in the other armchair. We all were looking down at our shoes, like they contained the secret to the universe.

The doctor gave a little intro: We're here today to get some things out on the table. Move forward. Begin the healing process.

Wait, Dad said. I thought we were here to talk about him.

We're here to talk about your family dynamic.

Dad cracked a knuckle. I'm sorry. I can't do this.

Jon, Mom said.

No, really. Excuse me. I'll be in the car.

He got up and left.

The doctor turned to me. How do you feel about what your father just did?

I think he's a chicken-shit, I said.

And you? she asked my mother.

I'm glad he walked out, she said. Because now I can tell you how much I hate him.

Mom listed Dad's faults. He was controlling. Dictatorial. Angry. Moody. Sexually demanding.

Any pros? I finally interrupted.

Mom looked down at her hands. I love him.

You just said you hated him!

I wouldn't bother to hate Dad if I didn't love him.

That's sick, I said. And you wouldn't say shit like that about Dad if he were sitting here.

He isn't sitting here, Mom said, so I'll say whatever I please.

At the end of the fifty-minute hour—which actually ran a little over—Dad was hanging by the car. He looked at his watch.

You obviously had a lot to get off your chest, he told Mom.

I'm not going back there, I announced.

Maybe I'll keep your appointment, Mom said.

Dad looked furious—but I couldn't tell if he was mad at Mom, or me, or himself.

Let's see how well *you* steer the ship. He tossed me the car keys. Drive us home.

I got behind the wheel. Dad got into the back seat—where Jordy always sat—which left Mom up front with me.

Mom started coaching me: Make sure you buckle up, honey. Remember to adjust your mirrors.

Goddammit, Cat, Dad said, let him make his own mistakes.

My hands shook as I turned the key in the ignition. I gave the car too much gas and Mom winced as the engine roared. No sooner did I take the car out of park than I made my first mistake. I put the car in drive rather than reverse; it jolted forward and I hit the brakes. I heard Jordy's voice: *Reverse, you dumb fuck!* My throat was dry, and Mom's foot was on an imaginary brake as I backed out the car—almost hitting the shrink's Jag—then peeled out of the parking lot.

At first, I couldn't get the hang of keeping a constant speed, and I definitely didn't have the feel of the brakes. I got honked at twice. When we got on Sheridan Road, where the lights were timed for optimum traffic flow, I started to relax and it was just like riding a bike—all of a sudden, I was just doing it.

Typewriter

After dinner that night, Dad told me, Put on your jacket. We're going for a walk, you and me.

Dad and I turned right at the campus gates and headed toward the lake.

How are those pills working out for you? he asked.

All right.

You seem more like yourself since you started taking them. You feel better?

A little.

All right then.

What did Dad mean by that? I thought I would ask Mom, until I realized I was doing exactly what the shrink had told me not to do. Talk to your father, she had said. Each time you talk to him, you teach him how to talk back.

Can I stop taking the pills? I wanted to ask Dad. But he had already moved on, in his head, to another subject.

I was thinking, Dad said, maybe it would help for you to write about it.

What *it*?

Your feelings. About Jordy. Or about your family that can't *triangulate*—or whatever the fuck else that doctor of yours thinks is wrong with us.

So I don't have to go back to talking to her? I asked.

Not unless you enjoy spilling your guts out.

Mom sure did.

Do I want to know what she said in that doctor's office?

If you did, I said, you wouldn't have walked out on us.

I didn't walk out on you, Dad said. I walked out on myself.

When we got home, Dad parked his old Olivetti—one that Jordy used to love to peck at—on my desk.

I want to hear that typewriter going, he said. For fifteen minutes, half an hour a night.

Jordy was the writer, Dad.

He can't write his story now. So do it for him.

At first, I thought it would be hard to sit down at the typewriter every night. Yet just like driving, after a while it came easily. I made a list of all the fun stuff Jordy and I had done together:

building bridges with Tinkertoys and cabins with Lincoln Logs, jumping off the hayloft at the farm, chasing lambs around the pasture, shivering in the cold water of Lake Michigan. I started making a long list of things I'd already done without him: My first solo haircut. My first drive on the street. The first time my voice dropped—and stayed there.

Over the years that list grew and grew. I got my driver's license. My high school diploma. Got rejected by Harvard. Accepted—without a cent of financial aid—to University of Chicago. My first cigarette. My first beer. My first girl. Rome, Athens, Prague, Budapest. As the list got longer, it became easier and easier to feel like I had "moved on," until this past year, when the ground seemed to shift beneath our feet and the earth suddenly teemed again with insects. Then I remembered how much Jordy had loved the cicadas, and my heart hurt to know he never would hear them sing again.

Epilogue

Dear Mr. Christian Wild,

Thank you for your interest in participating in our research study on lone twins. Please check whichever statements pertain to you:

___*I am able to tell others that I once was part of a twin set.*

___*I speak about my deceased twin freely with others.*

___*I am able to look at pictures of my deceased twin without crying.*

___*I am able to wake up from a dream about my deceased twin without becoming unsettled.*

___*I am able to enjoy my own life without constantly thinking of what my deceased twin is missing.*

___I am able to look in the mirror without thinking of what my deceased twin would look like.

___I am able to enjoy my birthday even though my deceased twin is not there to enjoy it with me.

___I am able to function and meet ordinary responsibilities on the anniversary of my twin's death.

___I am able to enjoy holidays even though my deceased twin is not there to enjoy them with me.

___I am able to acknowledge my deceased twin to my parents.

___My parents are able to acknowledge my deceased twin to me.

_✓_I have found a way to memorialize my deceased twin that is meaningful for me.

—for my brother, Jordan

Acknowledgments

A section of this novella, under the title "It Ends the Way It Always Ends," previously appeared in *Lunch Ticket*. I'm grateful to the Ragdale Foundation and the Lake Forest Library for their support of this work and indebted to the many researchers and organizations devoted to the study of lone twins.

My thanks to John Cassels for his expert editing and to Joseph Chaney and the staff of Wolfson Press.

The Author

Rita Ciresi is author of the novels *Bring Back My Body to Me, Blue Italian, Pink Slip,* and *Remind Me Again Why I Married You;* the story collections *Sometimes I Dream in Italian* and *Mother Rocket;* and the flash fiction collections *Female Education* and *Second Wife*. Her honors include the Flannery O'Connor Award for Short Fiction, finalist for the *Los Angeles Times'* Art Seidenbaum Award for First Fiction, the Pirate's Alley Faulkner Prize for the Novel, and the Jeanne Leiby Chapbook Award.

Ciresi has received support from the state arts councils of Pennsylvania, Virginia, and Florida. She has been in residence at the American Academy in Rome, Hawthornden International Writers' Retreat, Sozopol Fiction Seminars, Martha's Vineyard Writers Residency, Virginia Center for the Arts, Atlantic Center for the Arts, Santa Fe Art Institute, and Helene Wurlitzer Foundation. She has written the first and final drafts of most of her work at the Ragdale Foundation.